QUICK!

MISCHIEF MAKERS,
SIGN HERE so everyone
knows **this book** belongs
TO YOU.

_____

ROALD DAHL was a spy, ace fighter pilot, chocolate historian and medical inventor. He was also the author of *Charlie and the Chocolate Factory*, *Matilda*, *The BFG* and many more brilliant stories. He remains

THE WORLD'S NUMBER ONE STORYTELLER.

QUENTIN BLAKE has illustrated more than three hundred books and was Roald Dahl's favourite illustrator. In 1980 he won the prestigious Kate Greenaway Medal. In 1999 he became the first ever Children's Laureate and in 2013 he was knighted for services to illustration.

INTRODUCING . . .

Mr
Twit

Mrs
Twit

The
Roly-Poly
Bird

The
Muggle-Wump
Monkeys

Books by Roald Dahl

THE BFG
BOY: TALES OF CHILDHOOD
BOY *and* GOING SOLO
CHARLIE AND THE CHOCOLATE FACTORY
CHARLIE AND THE GREAT GLASS ELEVATOR
THE COMPLETE ADVENTURES OF CHARLIE AND MR WILLY WONKA
DANNY THE CHAMPION OF THE WORLD
THE ENORMOUS CROCODILE
ESIO TROT
FANTASTIC MR FOX
GEORGE'S MARVELLOUS MEDICINE
THE GIRAFFE AND THE PELLY AND ME
GOING SOLO
JAMES AND THE GIANT PEACH
MATILDA
THE MAGIC FINGER
THE TWITS
THE WITCHES

Picture books

DIRTY BEASTS
THE ENORMOUS CROCODILE
THE GIRAFFE AND THE PELLY AND ME
THE MINPINS
REVOLTING RHYMES

Plays

THE BFG: PLAYS FOR CHILDREN (*Adapted by David Wood*)
CHARLIE AND THE CHOCOLATE FACTORY: A PLAY (*Adapted by Richard George*)
DANNY THE CHAMPION OF THE WORLD: PLAYS FOR CHILDREN
(*Adapted by David Wood*)
FANTASTIC MR FOX: A PLAY (*Adapted by Sally Reid*)
JAMES AND THE GIANT PEACH: A PLAY (*Adapted by Richard George*)
THE TWITS: PLAYS FOR CHILDREN (*Adapted by David Wood*)
THE WITCHES: PLAYS FOR CHILDREN (*Adapted by David Wood*)

Teenage fiction

THE GREAT AUTOMATIC GRAMMATIZATOR AND OTHER STORIES
RHYME STEW
SKIN AND OTHER STORIES
THE VICAR OF NIBBLESWICKE
THE WONDERFUL STORY OF HENRY SUGAR AND SIX MORE

Collections

THE ROALD DAHL TREASURY
SONGS AND VERSE

ROALD DAHL

THE TWITS

Illustrated by **Quentin Blake**

PUFFIN

Find out more about Roald Dahl
by visiting the website at
roalddahl.com

PUFFIN BOOKS

UK | USA | Canada | Ireland | Australia
India | New Zealand | South Africa

Puffin Books is part of the Penguin Random House group of companies
whose addresses can be found at global.penguinrandomhouse.com.

puffinbooks.com

First published by Jonathan Cape 1980
Published by Puffin Books 1982
This edition published 2016
012

Set in Baskerville MT 14/17 pt by Palimpsest Book Production Limited, Falkirk, Stirlingshire
Printed in Great Britain by Clays Ltd, Elcograf S.p.A.

A CIP catalogue record for this book is available from the British Library

ISBN: 978–0–141–37147–4

www.greenpenguin.co.uk

MIX
Paper from
responsible sources
FSC® C018179

Penguin Random House is committed to a
sustainable future for our business, our readers
and our planet. This book is made from Forest
Stewardship Council® certified paper.

For Emma

Contents

Hairy Faces

What a lot of hairy-faced men there are around nowadays.

When a man grows hair all over his face it is impossible to tell what he really looks like.

Perhaps that's why he does it. He'd rather you didn't know.

Then there's the problem of washing.

When the very hairy ones wash their faces, it must be as big a job as when you and I wash the hair on our heads.

So what I want to know is this. How often do all these hairy-faced men wash their faces? Is it only once a week, like us, on Sunday nights? And do they shampoo it? Do they use a hairdryer? Do they rub hair-tonic in to stop their faces from going bald? Do they go to a barber to have their hairy faces cut and trimmed or do they do it themselves in front of the bathroom mirror with nail-scissors?

I don't know. But next time you see a man with a hairy face (which will probably be as soon as you step out on to the street) maybe you will look at him more closely and start wondering about some of these things.

Mr Twit

Mr Twit was one of these very hairy-faced men. The whole of his face except for his forehead, his eyes and his nose was covered with thick hair. The stuff even sprouted in revolting tufts out of his nostrils and ear-holes.

Mr Twit felt that this hairiness made him look terrifically wise and grand. But in truth he was neither of these things. Mr Twit was a twit. He was born a twit. And now at the age of sixty, he was a bigger twit than ever.

The hair on Mr Twit's face didn't grow smooth and matted as it does on most hairy-faced men. It grew in spikes that stuck out straight like the bristles of a nailbrush.

And how often did Mr Twit wash this bristly nailbrushy face of his?

The answer is NEVER, not even on Sundays.

He hadn't washed it for years.

Dirty Beards

As you know, an ordinary unhairy face like yours or mine simply gets a bit smudgy if it is not washed often enough, and there's nothing so awful about that.

But a hairy face is a very different matter. Things *cling* to hairs, especially food. Things like gravy go right in among the hairs and stay there. You and I can wipe our smooth faces with a flannel and we quickly look more or less all right again, but the hairy man cannot do that.

We can also, if we are careful, eat our meals without spreading food all over our faces. But not so the hairy man. Watch carefully next time you see a hairy man eating his lunch and you will notice that even if he opens his mouth very wide, it is impossible for him to get a spoonful of beef-stew or ice-cream and chocolate sauce into it without leaving some of it on the hairs.

Mr Twit didn't even bother to open his mouth wide when he ate. As a result (and because he never washed) there were always hundreds of bits of old breakfasts and lunches and suppers sticking to the hairs around his face. They weren't big bits, mind you, because he used to wipe those off with the back of his hand or on his sleeve while he was eating. But if you looked closely (not that you'd ever want to) you would see tiny little specks of dried-up scrambled eggs stuck to the hairs, and spinach and tomato ketchup and fish fingers and minced chicken livers and all the other disgusting things Mr Twit liked to eat.

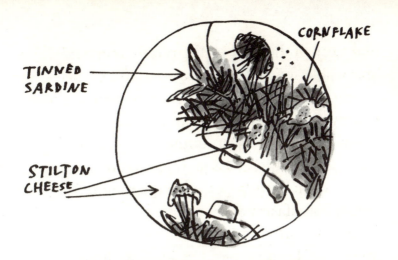

CORNFLAKE

TINNED SARDINE

STILTON CHEESE

If you looked closer still (hold your noses, ladies and gentlemen), if you peered deep into the moustachy bristles sticking out over his upper lip, you would probably see much larger objects that had escaped the wipe of his hand, things that had been there for months and months, like a piece of maggoty green cheese or a mouldy old cornflake or even the slimy tail of a tinned sardine.

Because of all this, Mr Twit never went really hungry. By sticking out his tongue and curling it sideways to explore the hairy jungle around his mouth, he was always able to find a tasty morsel here and there to nibble on.

What I am trying to tell you is that Mr Twit was a foul and smelly old man.

He was also an extremely horrid old man, as you will find out in a moment.

Mrs Twit

Mrs Twit was no better than her husband.

She did not, of course, have a hairy face. It was a pity she didn't because that at any rate would have hidden some of her fearful ugliness.

Take a look at her.

Have you ever seen a woman with an uglier face than that?

I doubt it. But the funny thing is that Mrs Twit wasn't born ugly. She'd had quite a nice face when she was young. The ugliness had grown upon her year by year as she got older.

Why would that happen? I'll tell you why.

If a person has ugly thoughts, it begins to show on the face. And when that person has ugly thoughts every day, every week, every year, the face gets uglier and uglier until it gets so ugly you can hardly bear to look at it.

A person who has good thoughts cannot ever be ugly. You can have a wonky nose and a crooked mouth and a double chin and stick-out teeth, but if you have good thoughts they will shine out of your face like sunbeams and you will always look lovely.

Nothing shone out of Mrs Twit's face.

In her right hand she carried a walking-stick. She used to tell people that this was because she had warts growing on the sole of her left foot and walking was painful. But the real reason she carried a stick was so that she could hit things with it, things like dogs and cats and small children.

And then there was the glass eye. Mrs Twit had a glass eye that was always looking the other way.

The Glass Eye

You can play a lot of tricks with a glass eye because you can take it out and pop it back in again any time you like. You can bet your life Mrs Twit knew all the tricks.

One morning she took out her glass eye and dropped it into Mr Twit's mug of beer when he wasn't looking.

Mr Twit sat there drinking the beer slowly. The froth made a white ring on the hairs around his mouth. He wiped the white froth on to his sleeve and wiped his sleeve on his trousers.

'You're plotting something,' Mrs Twit said, keeping her back turned so he wouldn't see that she had taken out her glass eye. 'Whenever you go all quiet like that I know very well you're plotting something.'

Mrs Twit was right. Mr Twit was plotting away like mad. He was trying to think up a really nasty trick he could play on his wife that day.

'You'd better be careful,' Mrs Twit said, 'because when I see you starting to plot, I watch you like a wombat.'

'Oh, do shut up, you old hag,' Mr Twit said. He went on drinking his beer, and his evil mind kept working away on the latest horrid trick he was going to play on the old woman.

Suddenly, as Mr Twit tipped the last drop of beer down his throat, he caught sight of Mrs Twit's awful glass eye staring up at him from the bottom of the mug. It made him jump.

'I told you I was watching you,' cackled Mrs Twit. 'I've got eyes everywhere so you'd better be careful.'

The Frog

To pay her back for the glass eye in his beer, Mr Twit decided he would put a frog in Mrs Twit's bed.

He caught a big one down by the pond and carried it back secretly in a box.

That night, when Mrs Twit was in the bathroom getting ready for bed, Mr Twit slipped the frog between her sheets. Then he got into his own bed and waited for the fun to begin.

Mrs Twit came back and climbed into her bed and put out the light. She lay there in the dark scratching her tummy. Her tummy was itching. Dirty old hags like her always have itchy tummies.

Then all at once she felt something cold and slimy crawling over her feet. She screamed.

'What's the matter with you?' Mr Twit said.

'Help!' screamed Mrs Twit, bouncing about. 'There's something in my bed!'

'I'll bet it's that Giant Skillywiggler I saw on the floor just now,' Mr Twit said.

'That *what?*' screamed Mrs Twit.

'I tried to kill it but it got away,' Mr Twit said. 'It's got teeth like screwdrivers!'

'Help!' screamed Mrs Twit. 'Save me! It's all over my feet!'

'It'll bite off your toes,' said Mr Twit.

Mrs Twit fainted.

Mr Twit got out of bed and fetched a jug of cold water. He poured the water over Mrs Twit's head to revive her. The frog crawled up from under the sheets to get near the water. It started jumping about on the pillow. Frogs love water. This one was having a good time.

When Mrs Twit came to, the frog had just jumped on to her face. This is not a nice thing to happen to anyone in bed at night. She screamed again.

'By golly it *is* a Giant Skillywiggler!' Mr Twit said. 'It'll bite off your nose.'

Mrs Twit leapt out of bed and flew downstairs and spent the night on the sofa. The frog went to sleep on her pillow.

The Wormy Spaghetti

The next day, to pay Mr Twit back for the frog trick, Mrs Twit sneaked out into the garden and dug up some worms. She chose big long ones and put them in a tin and carried the tin back to the house under her apron.

At one o'clock, she cooked spaghetti for lunch and she mixed the worms in with the spaghetti, but only on her husband's plate. The worms didn't show because everything was covered with tomato sauce and sprinkled with cheese.

'Hey, my spaghetti's moving!' cried Mr Twit, poking around in it with his fork.

'It's a new kind,' Mrs Twit said, taking a mouthful from her own plate which of course had no worms. 'It's called Squiggly Spaghetti. It's delicious. Eat it up while it's nice and hot.'

Mr Twit started eating, twisting the long tomato-covered strings around his fork and shovelling them into his mouth. Soon there was tomato sauce all over his hairy chin.

'It's not as good as the ordinary kind,' he said, talking with his mouth full. 'It's too squishy.'

'I find it very tasty,' Mrs Twit said. She was watching him from the other end of the table. It gave her great pleasure to watch him eating worms.

'I find it rather bitter,' Mr Twit said. 'It's got a distinctly bitter flavour. Buy the other kind next time.'

Mrs Twit waited until Mr Twit had eaten the whole plateful. Then she said, 'You want to know why your spaghetti was squishy?'

Mr Twit wiped the tomato sauce from his beard with a corner of the tablecloth. 'Why?' he said.

'And why it had a nasty bitter taste?'

'Why?' he said.

'Because it was *worms*!' cried Mrs Twit, clapping her hands and stamping her feet on the floor and rocking with horrible laughter.

The Funny Walking-stick

To pay Mrs Twit back for the worms in his spaghetti, Mr Twit thought up a really clever nasty trick.

One night, when the old woman was asleep, he crept out of bed and took her walking-stick downstairs to his workshed. There he stuck a tiny round piece of wood (no thicker than a penny) on to the bottom of the stick.

This made the stick longer, but the difference was so small, the next morning Mrs Twit didn't notice it.

The following night, Mr Twit stuck on another tiny bit of wood. Every night, he crept downstairs and added an extra tiny thickness of wood to the end of the walking-stick. He did it very neatly so that the extra bits looked like a part of the old stick.

Gradually, but oh so gradually, Mrs Twit's walking-stick was getting longer and longer.

Now when something is growing very slowly, it is almost impossible to notice it happening. You yourself, for example, are actually growing taller every day that goes by, but you wouldn't think it, would you? It's happening so slowly you can't even notice it from one week to the next.

It was the same with Mrs Twit's walking-stick. It was all so slow and gradual that she didn't notice how long it was getting even when it was halfway up to her shoulder.

'That stick's too long for you,' Mr Twit said to her one day.

'Why so it is!' Mrs Twit said, looking at the stick. 'I've had a feeling there was something wrong but I couldn't for the life of me think what it was.'

'There's something wrong all right,' Mr Twit said, beginning to enjoy himself.

'What *can* have happened?' Mrs Twit said, staring at her old walking-stick. 'It must suddenly have grown longer.'

'Don't be a fool!' Mr Twit said. 'How can a walking-stick possibly grow longer? It's made of dead wood, isn't it? Dead wood can't grow.'

'Then what on earth has happened?' cried Mrs Twit.

'It's not the stick, it's *you*!' said Mr Twit, grinning horribly. 'It's *you* that's getting *shorter*! I've been noticing it for some time now.'

'That's not true!' cried Mrs Twit.

'You're shrinking, woman!' said Mr Twit.

'It's not possible!'

'Oh yes it jolly well is,' said Mr Twit. 'You're shrinking fast! You're shrinking *dangerously* fast! Why, you must have shrunk at least a foot in the last few days!'

'Never!' she cried.

'Of course you have! Take a look at your stick, you old goat, and see how much you've shrunk in comparison! You've got the *shrinks*, that's what you've got! You've got the dreaded *shrinks*!'

Mrs Twit began to feel so trembly she had to sit down.

Mrs Twit Has the Shrinks

As soon as Mrs Twit sat down, Mr Twit pointed at her and shouted, 'There you are! You're sitting in your old chair and you've shrunk so much your feet aren't even touching the ground!'

Mrs Twit looked down at her feet and by golly the man was right. Her feet were not touching the ground.

Mr Twit, you see, had been just as clever with the chair as he'd been with the walking-stick. Every night when he had gone downstairs and stuck a little bit extra on to the stick, he had done the same to the four legs of Mrs Twit's chair.

'Just look at you sitting there in your same old chair,' he cried, 'and you've shrunk so much your feet are dangling in the air!'

Mrs Twit went white with fear.

'You've got the *shrinks*!' cried Mr Twit, pointing his finger at her like a pistol. 'You've got them badly! You've got the most terrible case of shrinks I've ever seen!'

Mrs Twit became so frightened she began to dribble. But Mr Twit, still remembering the worms in his spaghetti, didn't feel sorry for her at all. 'I suppose you know what *happens* to you when you get the shrinks?' he said.

'What?' gasped Mrs Twit. 'What happens?'

'Your head SHRINKS into your neck . . .

'And your neck SHRINKS into your body . . .

'And your body SHRINKS into your legs . . .

'And your legs SHRINK into your feet. And in the end there's nothing left except a pair of shoes and a bundle of old clothes.'

'I can't bear it!' cried Mrs Twit.

'It's a terrible disease,' said Mr Twit. 'The worst in the world.'

'How long have I got?' cried Mrs Twit. 'How long before I finish up as a bundle of old clothes and a pair of shoes?'

Mr Twit put on a very solemn face. 'At the rate you're going,' he said, shaking his head sadly, 'I'd say not more than ten or eleven days.'

'But isn't there *anything* we can do?' cried Mrs Twit.

'There's only one cure for the shrinks,' said Mr Twit.

'Tell me!' she cried. 'Oh, tell me quickly!'

'We'll have to hurry!' said Mr Twit.

'I'm ready. I'll hurry! I'll do anything you say!' cried Mrs Twit.

'You won't last long if you don't,' said Mr Twit, giving her another grizzly grin.

'What is it I must do?' cried Mrs Twit, clutching her cheeks.

'You've got to be *stretched*,' said Mr Twit.

Mrs Twit Gets a Stretching

Mr Twit led Mrs Twit outdoors where he had everything ready for the great stretching.

He had one hundred balloons and lots of string.

He had a gas cylinder for filling the balloons.

He had fixed an iron ring into the ground.

'Stand here,' he said, pointing to the iron ring. He then tied Mrs Twit's ankles to the iron ring.

When that was done, he began filling the balloons with gas. Each balloon was on a long string and when it was filled with gas it pulled on its string, trying to go up and up. Mr Twit tied the ends of the strings to the top half of Mrs Twit's body. Some he tied round her neck, some under her arms, some to her wrists and some even to her hair.

Soon there were fifty coloured balloons floating in the air above Mrs Twit's head.

'Can you feel them stretching you?' asked Mr Twit.

'I can! I can!' cried Mrs Twit. 'They're stretching me like mad.'

He put on another ten balloons. The upward pull became very strong.

Mrs Twit was quite helpless now. With her feet

tied to the ground and her arms pulled upwards by the balloons, she was unable to move. She was a prisoner, and Mr Twit had intended to go away and leave her like that for a couple of days and nights to teach her a lesson. In fact, he was just about to leave when Mrs Twit opened her big mouth and said something silly.

'Are you sure my feet are tied properly to the ground?' she gasped. 'If those strings around my ankles break, it'll be goodbye for me!'

And that's what gave Mr Twit his second nasty idea.

Mrs Twit Goes Ballooning Up

'There's enough pull here to take me to the moon!' Mrs Twit cried out.

'To take you to *the moon!*' exclaimed Mr Twit. 'What a ghastly thought! We wouldn't want anything like that to happen, oh dear me no!'

'We most certainly wouldn't!' cried Mrs Twit. 'Put some more string around my ankles quickly! I want to feel absolutely safe!'

'Very well, my angel,' said Mr Twit, and with a

ghoulish grin on his lips he knelt down at her feet. He took a knife from his pocket and with one quick slash he cut through the strings holding Mrs Twit's ankles to the iron ring.

She went up like a rocket.

'Help!' she screamed. 'Save me!'

But there was no saving her now. In a few seconds she was high up in the blue sky and climbing fast.

Mr Twit stood below looking up. '*What* a pretty sight!' he said to himself. 'How lovely all those balloons look in the sky! And what a marvellous bit of luck for me! At last the old hag is lost and gone for ever.'

Mrs Twit Comes Ballooning Down

Mrs Twit may have been ugly and she may have been beastly, but she was not stupid.

High up there in the sky, she had a bright idea. 'If I can get rid of some of these balloons,' she said to herself, 'I will stop going up and start to come down.'

She began biting through the strings that held the balloons to her wrists and arms and neck and hair. Each time she bit through a string and let the balloon float away, the upward pull got less and her rate of climb slowed down.

When she had bitten through twenty strings, she stopped going up altogether. She stayed still in the air.

She bit through one more string.

Very, very slowly, she began to float downwards.

It was a calm day. There was no wind at all. And because of this, Mrs Twit had gone absolutely straight up. She now began to come absolutely straight down.

As she floated gently down, Mrs Twit's petticoat billowed out like a parachute, showing her long knickers. It was a grand sight on a glorious day, and thousands of birds came flying in from miles around to stare at this extraordinary old woman in the sky.

Mr Twit Gets a Horrid Shock

Mr Twit, who thought he had seen his ugly wife for the last time, was sitting in the garden celebrating with a mug of beer.

Silently, Mrs Twit came floating down. When she was about the height of the house above Mr Twit, she suddenly called out at the top of her voice, 'Here I come, you grizzly old grunion! You rotten old turnip! You filthy old frumpet!'

Mr Twit jumped as though he'd been stung by a giant wasp. He dropped his beer. He looked up. He gaped. He gasped. He gurgled. A few choking sounds came out of his mouth. '*Ughhhhhhhh!*' he said. '*Arghhhhhhhh! Ouchhhhhhhh!*'

'I'll get you for this!' shouted Mrs Twit. She was floating down right on top of him. She was purple with rage and slashing the air with her long walking-stick which she had somehow managed to hang on to all the time. 'I'll swish you to a swazzle!' she shouted. 'I'll swash you to a swizzle! I'll gnash you to a gnozzle! I'll gnosh you to a gnazzle!' And before Mr Twit had time to run away, this bundle of balloons and petticoats and fiery fury landed right on top of him, lashing out with the stick and cracking him all over his body.

The House, the Tree and the Monkey Cage

But that's enough of that. We can't go on forever watching these two disgusting people doing disgusting things to each other. We must get ahead with the story.

Here is a picture of Mr and Mrs Twit's house and garden. Some house! It looks like a prison. And not a window anywhere.

'Who wants windows?' Mr Twit had said when they were building it. 'Who wants every Tom, Dick and Harry peeping in to see what you're doing?' It didn't occur to Mr Twit that windows were meant mainly for looking out of, not for looking into.

And what do you think of that ghastly garden? Mrs Twit was the gardener. She was very good at growing thistles and stinging-nettles. 'I always grow plenty of spiky thistles and plenty of stinging-nettles,' she used to say. 'They keep out nasty nosey little children.'

Near the house you can see Mr Twit's work-shed.

To one side there is The Big Dead Tree. It never has any leaves on it because it's dead.

And not far from the tree, you can see the monkey cage. There are four monkeys in it. They belong to Mr Twit. You will hear about them later.

Hugtight Sticky Glue

Once a week, on Wednesdays, the Twits had Bird Pie for supper. Mr Twit caught the birds and Mrs Twit cooked them.

Mr Twit was good at catching birds. On the day before Bird Pie day, he would put the ladder up against The Big Dead Tree and climb into the branches with a bucket of glue and a paint-brush. The glue he used was something called HUGTIGHT and it was stickier than any other glue in the world. He would paint it along the tops of all the branches and then go away.

As the sun went down, birds would fly in from all

around to roost for the night in The Big Dead Tree. They didn't know, poor things, that the branches were all smeared with horrible HUGTIGHT. The moment they landed on a branch, their feet stuck and that was that.

The next morning, which was Bird Pie day, Mr Twit would climb up the ladder again and grab all the wretched birds that were stuck to the tree. It didn't matter what kind they were – song thrushes, blackbirds, sparrows, crows, little jenny wrens, robins, anything – they all went into the pot for Wednesday's Bird Pie supper.

Four Sticky Little Boys

On one Tuesday evening after Mr Twit had been up the ladder and smeared the tree with HUGTIGHT, four little boys crept into the garden to look at the monkeys. They didn't care about the thistles and stinging-nettles, not when there were monkeys to look at. After a while, they got tired of looking at the monkeys, so they explored further into the garden and found the ladder leaning against The Big Dead Tree. They decided to climb up it just for fun.

There's nothing wrong with that.

The next morning, when Mr Twit went out to collect the birds, he found four miserable little boys sitting in the tree, stuck as tight as could be by the seats of their pants to the branches. There were no birds because the presence of the boys had scared them away.

Mr Twit was furious. 'As there are no birds for my pie tonight,' he shouted, 'then it'll have to be *boys* instead!' He started to climb the ladder. 'Boy Pie might be better than Bird Pie,' he went on, grinning horribly. 'More meat and not so many tiny little bones!'

The boys were terrified. 'He's going to boil us!' cried one of them.

'He'll stew us alive!' wailed the second one.

'He'll cook us with carrots!' cried the third.

But the fourth little boy, who had more sense than the others, whispered, 'Listen, I've just had an idea. We are only stuck by *the seats of our pants*. So quick! Unbutton your pants and slip out of them and fall to the ground.'

Mr Twit had reached the top of the ladder and was just about to make a grab for the nearest boy when they all suddenly tumbled out of the tree and ran for home with their naked bottoms winking at the sun.

The Great Upside Down Monkey Circus

Now for the monkeys.

The four monkeys in the cage in the garden were all one family. They were Muggle-Wump and his wife and their two small children. But what on earth were Mr and Mrs Twit doing with monkeys in their garden?

Well, in the old days, they had both worked in a circus as monkey trainers. They used to teach monkeys to do tricks and to dress up in human clothes and to smoke pipes and all the rest of that nonsense.

Today, although they were retired, Mr Twit still wanted to train monkeys. It was his dream that one day he would own the first GREAT UPSIDEDOWN MONKEY CIRCUS in the world.

That meant that the monkeys had to do everything upside down. They had to dance upside down (on their hands with their feet in the air). They had to play football upside down. They had to balance one on top of the other upside down, with Muggle-Wump at the bottom and the smallest baby monkey at the very top. They even had to eat and drink upside down and that is not an easy thing to do because the food and water has to go *up* your throat instead of down it. In fact, it is almost impossible, but the monkeys simply had to do it otherwise they got nothing.

All this sounds pretty silly to you and me. It sounded pretty silly to the monkeys, too. They absolutely hated having to do this upside down nonsense day after day. It made them giddy standing on their heads for hours on end. Sometimes the two small monkey children would faint with so much blood going to their heads. But Mr Twit didn't care about that. He kept them practising for six hours every day and if they didn't do as they were told, Mrs Twit would soon come running with her beastly stick.

The Roly-Poly Bird
to the Rescue

Muggle-Wump and his family longed to escape from the cage in Mr Twit's garden and go back to the African jungle where they came from.

They hated Mr and Mrs Twit for making their lives so miserable.

They also hated them for what they did to the birds every Tuesday and Wednesday. 'Fly away, birds!' they used to shout, jumping about in the cage and waving their arms. 'Don't sit on that Big Dead Tree! It's just been smeared all over with sticky glue! Go and sit somewhere else!'

But these were English birds and they couldn't understand the weird African language the monkeys spoke. So they took no notice and went on using The Big Dead Tree and getting caught for Mrs Twit's Bird Pie.

Then one day, a truly magnificent bird flew down out of the sky and landed on the monkey cage.

'Good heavens!' cried all the monkeys together. 'It's the Roly-Poly Bird! What on earth are you doing over here in England, Roly-Poly Bird?' Like the monkeys, the Roly-Poly Bird came from Africa and he spoke the same language as they did.

'I've come for a holiday,' said the Roly-Poly Bird. 'I like to travel.' He fluffed his marvellous coloured feathers and looked down rather grandly at the monkeys. 'For most people,' he went on, 'flying away on holiday is very expensive, but I can fly anywhere in the world for nothing.'

'Do you know how to talk to these English birds?' Muggle-Wump asked him.

'Of course I do,' said the Roly-Poly Bird. 'It's no good going to a country and not knowing the language.'

'Then we must hurry,' said Muggle-Wump. 'Today is Tuesday and over there you can already see the revolting Mr Twit up the ladder painting sticky glue on all the branches of The Big Dead Tree. This evening when the birds come in to roost, you must warn them not to perch on that tree or they will be made into Bird Pie.'

That evening, the Roly-Poly Bird flew round and round The Big Dead Tree singing out,

'There's sticky stick stuff all over the tree!
If you land in the branches, you'll never get free!
So fly away! Fly away! Stay up high!
Or you'll finish up tomorrow in a hot Bird Pie!'

No Bird Pie for Mr Twit

The next morning when Mr Twit came out with his huge basket to snatch all the birds from The Big Dead Tree, there wasn't a single one on it. They were all sitting on top of the monkey cage. The Roly-Poly Bird was there as well, and Muggle-Wump and his family were inside the cage and the whole lot of them were laughing at Mr Twit.

Still No Bird Pie for Mr Twit

Mr Twit wasn't going to wait another week for his Bird Pie supper. He loved Bird Pie. It was his favourite meal. So that very same day, he went after the birds again. This time he smeared all the top bars of the monkey cage with sticky glue, as well as the branches of The Big Dead Tree. 'Now I'll get you,' he said, 'whichever one you sit on!'

The monkeys crouched inside the cage watching all this, and later on, when the Roly-Poly Bird came swooping in for an evening chat, they shouted out, 'Don't land on our cage, Roly-Poly Bird! It's covered in sticky glue! So is the tree!'

And that evening, as the sun went down and all the birds came in again to roost, the Roly-Poly Bird flew round and round the monkey cage and The Big Dead Tree, singing out his warning,

'There's sticky stuff now on the cage *and* the tree!
If you land on either, you'll never get free!
So fly away! Fly away! Stay up high!
Or you'll finish up tomorrow in a hot Bird Pie!'

Mr and Mrs Twit
Go Off to Buy Guns

The next morning when Mr Twit came out with his huge basket, not a single bird was sitting on either the monkey cage or The Big Dead Tree. They were all perched happily on the roof of Mr Twit's house. The Roly-Poly Bird was up there as well, and the monkeys were in the cage and the whole lot of them were hooting with laughter at Mr Twit.

'I'll wipe that silly laugh off your beaks!' Mr Twit screamed at the birds. 'I'll get you next time, you filthy feathery frumps! I'll wring your necks, the whole lot of you, and have you bubbling in the pot for Bird Pie before this day is out!'

'How are you going to do that?' asked Mrs Twit, who had come outside to see what all the noise was about. 'I won't have you smearing sticky glue all over the roof of our house!'

Mr Twit got very excited. 'I've got a great idea!' he cried. He didn't bother to keep his voice down because he didn't think the monkeys could understand. 'We'll both go into town right away and we'll buy a gun each!' he shouted. 'How's that?'

'Brilliant!' cried Mrs Twit, grinning and showing her long yellow teeth. 'We'll buy those big shotguns that spray out fifty bullets or more with each bang!'

'Exactly,' said Mr Twit. 'Lock up the house while I go and make sure the monkeys are safely shut away.'

Mr Twit went over to the monkey cage. 'Attention!' he barked in his fearsome monkey-trainer's voice. 'Upside down all of you and jump to it! One on top of the other! Quick! Get on with it or you'll feel Mrs Twit's stick across your backsides!'

Obediently, the poor monkeys stood on their hands and clambered one on top of the other, with Muggle-Wump at the bottom and the smallest child at the very top.

'Now stay there till we come back!' Mr Twit ordered. 'Don't you dare to move! And don't overbalance! When we return in two or three hours' time, I shall expect to find you all in exactly the same position as you are now! You understand?'

With that, Mr Twit marched away. Mrs Twit went with him. And the monkeys were left alone with the birds.

Muggle-Wump Has an Idea

As soon as Mr and Mrs Twit had disappeared down the road, the monkeys all flipped back on to their feet the right way up. 'Quick, get the key!' Muggle-Wump called out to the Roly-Poly Bird, who was still sitting on the roof of the house.

'What key?' shouted the Roly-Poly Bird. 'The key to the door of our cage,' cried Muggle-Wump. 'It's hanging on a nail in the workshed. That's where he always puts it.'

The Roly-Poly Bird flew down and came back with the key in his beak. Muggle-Wump reached a

hand through the bars of the cage and took the key.

He put it in the lock and turned it. The door opened. All four monkeys leapt out together.

'We are free!' cried the two little ones. 'Where shall we go, Dad? Where shall we hide?'

'Don't get excited,' said Muggle-Wump. 'Calm down, everybody. Before we escape from this beastly place we have one very important thing to do.'

'What?' they asked him.

'We're going to turn those terrible Twits UPSIDE DOWN!'

'We're going to *what?*' they cried. 'You must be joking, Dad!'

'I'm not joking,' Muggle-Wump said. 'We're going to turn both Mr and Mrs Twit UPSIDE DOWN with their legs in the air!'

'Don't be ridiculous,' the Roly-Poly Bird said. 'How can we possibly turn those two maggoty old monsters upside down?'

'We can, we can!' cried Muggle-Wump. 'We are going to make them stand on their heads for hours and hours! Perhaps for ever! Let *them* see what it feels like for a change!'

'How?' said the Roly-Poly Bird. 'Just tell me how.'

Muggle-Wump laid his head on one side and a

tiny twinkling little smile touched the corners of his mouth. 'Now and again,' he said, 'but not very often, I have a brilliant idea. This is one of them. Follow me, my friends, follow me.' He scampered off towards the house and the three other monkeys and the Roly-Poly Bird went after him.

'Buckets and paint-brushes!' cried Muggle-Wump. 'That's what we want next! There are plenty in the workshed! Hurry up, everyone! Get a bucket and a paint-brush!'

Inside Mr Twit's workshed there was an enormous barrel of HUGTIGHT sticky glue, the stuff he used for catching birds. 'Fill your buckets!' Muggle-Wump ordered. 'We are now going into the big house!'

Mrs Twit had hidden the key to the front door under the mat and Muggle-Wump had seen her doing it, so it was easy for them to get in. In they went, all four monkeys, with their buckets of sticky glue. Then came the Roly-Poly Bird flying in after them, with a bucket in his beak and a brush in his claw.

The Great Glue
Painting Begins

'This is the living-room,' announced Muggle-Wump. 'The grand and glorious living-room where those two fearful frumptious freaks eat Bird Pie every week for supper!'

'Please don't mention Bird Pie again,' said the Roly-Poly Bird. 'It gives me the shudders.'

'We mustn't waste time!' cried Muggle-Wump. 'Hurry up, hurry up! Now the first thing is this! I want everyone to paint sticky glue all over the ceiling! Cover it all! Smear it in every corner!'

'Over the ceiling!' they cried. 'Why the *ceiling*?'

'Never mind why!' shouted Muggle-Wump. 'Just do as you're told and don't argue!'

'But how do we get *up* there?' they asked. 'We can't reach.'

'Monkeys can reach anywhere!' shouted Muggle-Wump. He was in a frenzy of excitement now, waving his paint-brush and his bucket and leaping about all over the room. 'Come on, come on! Jump on the table! Stand on the chairs! Hop on each other's shoulders! Roly-Poly can do it flying! Don't stand there gaping! We have to hurry, don't you understand that? Those terrible Twits will be back any moment and this time they'll have *guns*! Get on with it, for heaven's sake! Get on with it!'

And so the great glue painting of the ceiling began. All the other birds who had been sitting on the roof flew in to help, carrying paint-brushes in their claws and beaks. There were buzzards,

magpies, rooks, ravens and many
more. Everyone was splashing away
like mad and, with so many helpers,
the job was soon finished.

The Carpet Goes
on the Ceiling

'What now?' they all said, looking at Muggle-Wump.

'Ah-ha!' cried Muggle-Wump. 'Now for the fun! Now for the greatest upside down trick of all time! Are you ready?'

'We're ready,' said the monkeys. 'We're ready,' said the birds.

'Pull out the carpet!' shouted Muggle-Wump. 'Pull this huge carpet out from under the furniture and stick it on to the ceiling!'

'On to the *ceiling*!' cried one of the small monkeys. 'But that's impossible, Dad!'

'I'll stick *you* on to the ceiling if you don't shut up!' snapped Muggle-Wump.

'He's dotty!' they cried.

'He's barmy!'

'He's batty!'

'He's nutty!'

'He's screwy!'

'He's wacky!' cried the Roly-Poly Bird. 'Poor old Muggles has gone off his wump at last!'

'Oh, do stop shouting such rubbish and give me a hand,' said Muggle-Wump, catching hold of one corner of the carpet. 'Pull, you nitwits, pull!'

The carpet was enormous. It covered the entire

floor from wall to wall. It had a red and gold pattern on it. It is not easy to pull an enormous carpet off the floor when the room is full of tables and chairs. 'Pull!' yelled Muggle-Wump. 'Pull, pull, pull!' He was like a demon hopping round the room and telling everyone what to do. But you couldn't blame him. After months and months of standing on his head with his family, he couldn't wait for the time when the terrible Twits would be doing the same thing. At least that's what he hoped.

With the monkeys and the birds all pulling and puffing, the carpet was dragged off the floor and finally hoisted up on to the ceiling. And there it stuck.

All at once, the whole ceiling of the living-room was carpeted in red and gold.

The Furniture Goes Up

'Now the table, the big table!' shouted Muggle-Wump. 'Turn the table upside down and put a dollop of sticky glue on to the bottom of each leg. Then we shall stick that on to the ceiling as well!'

Hoisting the huge table upside down on to the ceiling was not an easy job, but they managed it in the end.

'Will it stay there?' they cried. 'Is the glue strong enough to hold it up?'

'It's the strongest glue in the world!' Muggle-Wump replied. 'It's the special bird-catching bird-killing glue for smearing on trees!'

'Please,' said the Roly-Poly Bird. 'I have asked you before not to mention that subject. How would *you* like it if it was Monkey Pie they made every Wednesday and all your friends had been boiled up and I went on talking about it?'

'I do beg your pardon,' said Muggle-Wump. 'I'm so excited I hardly know what I'm saying. Now the chairs! Do the same with the chairs! All the chairs must be stuck upside down to the ceiling! And in

their right places! Oh, do hurry up, everybody! Any moment now, those two filthy freaks are going to come rushing in with their guns!'

The monkeys, with the birds helping them, put glue on the bottom of each chair leg and hoisted them up to the ceiling.

'Now the smaller tables!' shouted Muggle-Wump. 'And the big sofa! And the sideboard! And the lamps! And all the tiny little things! The ashtrays! The ornaments! And that beastly plastic gnome on the sideboard! Everything, absolutely everything must be stuck to the ceiling!'

It was terribly hard work. It was especially difficult to stick everything on to the ceiling in exactly its right place. But they got it done in the end.

'What now?' asked the Roly-Poly Bird. He was out of breath and so tired he could hardly flap his wings.

'Now the pictures!' cried Muggle-Wump. 'Turn all the pictures upside down! And will one of you birds please fly out on to the road and watch to see when those frumptious freaks are coming back.'

'I'll go,' said the Roly-Poly Bird. 'I'll sit on the telephone wires and keep guard. It'll give me a rest.'

The Ravens Swoop Over

They had only just finished the job when the Roly-Poly Bird came swooping in, screaming, 'They're coming back! They're coming back!'

Quickly, the birds flew back on to the roof of the house. The monkeys rushed into their cage and stood upside down one on top of the other. A moment later, Mr and Mrs Twit came marching into the garden, each carrying a fearsome-looking gun.

'I'm glad to see those monkeys are still upside down,' said Mr Twit.

'They're too stupid to do anything else,' said Mrs Twit. 'Hey, look at all those cheeky birds still up

there on the roof! Let's go inside and load our lovely new guns and then it'll be *bang bang bang* and Bird Pie for supper.'

Just as Mr and Mrs Twit were about to enter the house, two black ravens swooped low over their heads. Each bird carried a paint-brush in its claw and each paint-brush was smeared with sticky glue. As the ravens whizzed over, they brushed a streak of sticky glue on to the tops of Mr and Mrs Twit's heads. They did it with the lightest touch but even so the Twits both felt it.

'What was *that*?' cried Mrs Twit. 'Some beastly bird has dropped his dirty droppings on my head!'

'On mine too!' shouted Mr Twit. 'I felt it! I felt it!'

'Don't touch it!' cried Mrs Twit. 'You'll get it all

over your hands! Come inside and we'll wash it off at the sink!'

'The filthy dirty brutes,' yelled Mr Twit. 'I'll bet they did it on purpose! Just wait till I've loaded up my gun!'

Mrs Twit got the key from under the doormat (where Muggle-Wump had carefully replaced it) and into the house they went.

The Twits Are Turned
Upside Down

'*What's this?*' gasped Mr Twit as they entered the living-room.

'*What's happened?*' screamed Mrs Twit.

They stood in the middle of the room, looking up. All the furniture, the big table, the chairs, the sofa, the lamps, the little side tables, the cabinet with bottles of beer in it, the ornaments, the electric fire, the carpet, everything was stuck upside down to the ceiling. The pictures were upside down on the walls. And the floor they were standing on was absolutely bare. What's more, it had been painted white to look like the ceiling.

'*Look!*' screamed Mrs Twit. '*That's the floor! The floor's up there! This is the ceiling! We are standing on the ceiling!*'

'We're UPSIDE DOWN!' gasped Mr Twit. 'We *must* be upside down. We are standing on the ceiling looking down at the floor!'

'Oh help!' screamed Mrs Twit. 'Help help help! I'm beginning to feel giddy!'

'So am I! So am I!' cried Mr Twit. 'I don't like this one little bit!'

'We're upside down and all the blood's going to my head!' screamed Mrs Twit. 'If we don't do something quickly, I shall die, I know I will!'

'I've got it!' cried Mr Twit. 'I know what we'll do! *We'll stand on our heads, then anyway we'll be the right way up!*'

So they stood on their heads, and of course, the moment the tops of their heads touched the floor, the sticky glue that the ravens had brushed on a few moments before did its job. They were stuck. They were pinned down, cemented, glued, fixed to the floorboards.

Through a crack in the door the monkeys watched. They'd jumped right out of their cage the moment the Twits had gone inside. And the Roly-Poly Bird watched. And all the other birds flew in and out to catch a glimpse of this extraordinary sight.

The Monkeys Escape

That evening, Muggle-Wump and his family went up to the big wood on top of the hill, and in the tallest tree of all they built a marvellous tree-house. All the birds, especially the big ones, the crows and

rooks and magpies, made their nests around the tree-house so that nobody could see it from the ground.

'You can't stay up here for ever, you know,' the Roly-Poly Bird said.

'Why not?' asked Muggle-Wump. 'It's a lovely place.'

'Just you wait till the winter comes,' the Roly-Poly Bird said. 'Monkeys don't like cold weather, do they?'

'They most certainly don't!' cried Muggle-Wump. 'Are the winters so very cold over here?'

'It's all snow and ice,' said the Roly-Poly Bird. 'Sometimes it's so cold a bird will wake up in the morning with his feet frozen to the bough that he's been roosting on.'

'Then what shall we do?' cried Muggle-Wump. 'My family will all be deep-freezed!'

'No, they won't,' said the Roly-Poly Bird. 'Because when the first leaves start falling from the trees in the autumn, you can all fly home to Africa with me.'

'Don't be ridiculous,' Muggle-Wump said. 'Monkeys can't fly.'

'You can sit on my back,' said the Roly-Poly Bird. 'I shall take you one at a time. You will travel by the Roly-Poly Super Jet and it won't cost you a penny!'

The Twits Get the Shrinks

And down here in the horrid house, Mr and Mrs Twit are still stuck upside down to the floor of the living-room.

'It's all your fault!' yelled Mr Twit, thrashing his legs in the air. '*You're* the one, you ugly old cow, who went hopping around shouting, "We're upside down! We're upside down!"'

'And *you're* the one who said to stand on our heads so we'd be the right way up, you whiskery old warthog!' screamed Mrs Twit. 'Now we'll never get free! We're stuck here for ever!'

'*You* may be stuck here for ever,' said Mr Twit. 'But not me! I'm going to get away!'

Mr Twit wriggled and squirmed, and he squiggled and wormed, and he twisted and turned, and he choggled and churned, but the sticky glue held him to the floor just as tightly as it had once held the poor birds in The Big Dead Tree. He was still as upside down as ever, standing on his head.

But heads are not made to be stood upon. If you stand on your head for a very long time, a horrid thing happens, and this was where Mr Twit got his biggest shock of all. With so much weight on it from up above, his head began to get squashed into his body.

Quite soon, it had disappeared completely, sunk out of sight in the fatty folds of his flabby neck.

'I'm SHRINKING!' burbled Mr Twit.

'So am I!' cried Mrs Twit.

'Help me! Save me! Call a doctor!' yelled Mr Twit. 'I'm getting THE DREADED SHRINKS!'

And so he was. Mrs Twit was getting THE DREADED SHRINKS, too! And this time it wasn't a fake. It was the real thing!

Their heads SHRANK into their necks . . .

Then their necks began SHRINKING into their bodies . . .

And their bodies began SHRINKING into their legs . . .

And their legs began SHRINKING into their feet . . .

And one week later, on a nice sunny afternoon, a man called Fred came round to read the gas meter. When nobody answered the door, Fred peeped into the house and there he saw, on the floor of the living-room, two bundles of old clothes, two pairs of shoes and a walking-stick. There was nothing more left in this world of Mr and Mrs Twit.

And everyone, including Fred, shouted . . . 'HOORAY!'

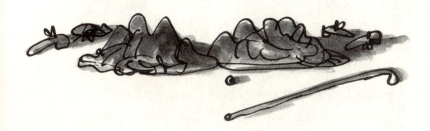

Turn the page to meet another terrible twosome, James's horrid Aunt Sponge and Aunt Spiker . . .

JAMES AND THE GIANT PEACH

Until he was four years old, James Henry Trotter had a happy life. He lived peacefully with his mother and father in a beautiful house beside the sea. There were always plenty of other children for him to play with, and there was the sandy beach for him to run about on, and the ocean to paddle in. It was the perfect life for a small boy.

Then, one day, James's mother and father went to London to do some shopping, and there a terrible thing happened. Both of them suddenly got eaten up (in full daylight, mind you, and on a crowded street) by an enormous angry rhinoceros which had escaped from the London Zoo.

Now this, as you can well imagine, was a rather nasty experience for two such gentle parents. But in the long run it was far nastier for James than it was for them. *Their* troubles were all over in a jiffy. They were dead and gone in thirty-five seconds flat. Poor James, on the other hand, was still very much alive, and all at once he found himself alone and frightened in a vast unfriendly world. The lovely house by the seaside had to be sold immediately, and the little boy, carrying nothing but a small suitcase containing a pair of pyjamas and a toothbrush, was sent away to live with his two aunts.

Their names were Aunt Sponge and Aunt Spiker, and I am sorry to say that they were both really horrible people. They were selfish and lazy and cruel, and right from the beginning they started beating poor James for almost no reason at all. They never called him by his real name, but always referred to him as 'you disgusting little beast' or 'you filthy nuisance' or 'you miserable creature', and they certainly never gave him any toys to play with or any picture books to look at. His room was as bare as a prison cell.

They lived – Aunt Sponge, Aunt Spiker, and now James as well – in a queer ramshackle house on the top of a high hill in the south of England. The hill was so high that from almost anywhere in the garden James could look down and see for miles and miles across a marvellous landscape of woods and fields; and on a very clear day, if he looked in the right direction, he could see a tiny grey dot far away on the horizon, which was the house that he used to live in with his beloved mother and father. And just beyond that, he could see the ocean itself – a long thin streak of blackish-blue, like a line of ink, beneath the rim of the sky.

But James was never allowed to go down off the top of that hill. Neither Aunt Sponge nor Aunt Spiker could ever be bothered to take him out herself, not even for a small walk or a picnic, and he certainly wasn't permitted to go alone. 'The nasty little beast will only get into mischief if he goes out of the garden,' Aunt Spiker had said. And terrible punishments were promised him, such as being locked up in the cellar with the rats for a week, if he even so much as dared to climb over the fence.

The garden, which covered the whole of the top of the hill, was large and desolate, and the only tree in the entire place (apart from a clump of dirty old laurel bushes at the far end) was an ancient peach tree that never gave any peaches. There was no swing, no seesaw, no sand pit, and no other children were ever invited to come up the hill to play with poor James. There wasn't so much as a dog or a cat around

to keep him company. And as time went on, he became sadder and sadder, and more and more lonely, and he used to spend hours every day standing at the bottom of the garden, gazing wistfully at the lovely but forbidden world of woods and fields and ocean that was spread out below him like a magic carpet.

After James Henry Trotter had been living with his aunts for three whole years there came a morning when something rather peculiar happened to him. And this thing, which as I say was only *rather* peculiar, soon caused a second thing to happen which was *very* peculiar. And then the *very* peculiar thing, in its own turn, caused a really *fantastically* peculiar thing to occur.

It all started on a blazing hot day in the middle of summer. Aunt Sponge, Aunt Spiker and James were all out in the garden. James had been put to work, as usual. This time he was chopping wood for the kitchen stove. Aunt Sponge and Aunt Spiker were sitting comfortably in deck-chairs near by, sipping tall glasses of fizzy lemonade and watching him to see that he didn't stop work for one moment.

Aunt Sponge was enormously fat and very short. She had small piggy eyes, a sunken mouth, and one of those white flabby faces that looked exactly as though it had been boiled. She was like a great white soggy overboiled cabbage. Aunt Spiker, on the other hand, was lean and tall and bony, and she wore steel-rimmed spectacles that fixed on to the end of her nose with a clip. She had a screeching voice and long wet narrow lips, and whenever she got angry or excited, little flecks of spit would come shooting out of her mouth as she talked. And there they sat, these two ghastly hags, sipping their drinks, and every now and again screaming at James to chop faster and faster. They also talked about themselves, each one saying how beautiful she thought she was.

Aunt Sponge had a long-handled mirror on her lap, and she kept picking it up and gazing at her own hideous face.

'I look and smell,' Aunt Sponge declared, 'as lovely as
*   a rose!*
Just feast your eyes upon my face, observe my shapely
*   nose!*
Behold my heavenly silky locks!
And if I take off both my socks
You'll see my dainty toes.'
'But don't forget,' Aunt Spiker cried, 'how much your
*   tummy shows!'*

Aunt Sponge went red. Aunt Spiker said, 'My sweet,
*   you cannot win,*
Behold MY gorgeous curvy shape, my teeth, my
*   charming grin!*
Oh, beauteous me! How I adore
My radiant looks! And please ignore
The pimple on my chin.'
'My dear old trout!' Aunt Sponge cried out. 'You're
*   only bones and skin!'*

'Such loveliness as I possess can only truly shine
In Hollywood!' Aunt Sponge declared: 'Oh, wouldn't
*   that be fine!*
I'd capture all the nations' hearts!
They'd give me all the leading parts!
The stars would all resign!'
'I think you'd make,' Aunt Spiker said, 'a lovely
*   Frankenstein.'*

Poor James was still slaving away at the chopping-block. The heat was terrible. He was sweating all over. His arm was aching. The chopper was a large blunt thing far too heavy for a small boy to use. And as he worked, James began thinking about all the other children in the world and what they might be doing at this moment. Some would be riding tricycles in their gardens. Some would be walking in cool woods and picking bunches of wild flowers. And all the little friends whom he used to know would be down by the seaside, playing in the wet sand and splashing around in the water . . .

Great tears began oozing out of James's eyes and rolling down his cheeks.

He stopped working and leaned against the chopping-block, overwhelmed by his own unhappiness.

'What's the matter with you?' Aunt Spiker screeched, glaring at him over the top of her steel spectacles.

James began to cry.

'Stop that immediately and get on with your work, you nasty little beast!' Aunt Sponge ordered.

'Oh, Auntie Sponge!' James cried out. 'And Auntie Spiker! Couldn't we all – *please* – just for once – go down to the seaside on the bus? It isn't very far – and I feel so hot and awful and lonely . . .'

'Why, you lazy good-for-nothing brute!' Aunt Spiker shouted.

'Beat him!' cried Aunt Sponge.

'I certainly will!' Aunt Spiker snapped. She glared at James, and James looked back at her with large frightened eyes. 'I shall beat you later on in the day when I don't feel so hot,' she said. 'And now get out of my sight, you disgusting little worm, and give me some peace!'

James turned and ran. He ran off as fast as he could to the far end of the garden and hid himself behind that clump of dirty old laurel bushes that we mentioned earlier on. Then he covered his face with his hands and began to cry and cry.

Have **YOU** PLAYED the **FANTASTICALLY** FUN **NEW** **ROALD DAHL** apps?

www.roalddahl.com/apps

ROALD DAHL DAY

CELEBRATE

THE **PHIZZ-WHIZZING**
WORLD of **ROALD DAHL**

EVERY YEAR on
13th SEPTEMBER!

JOIN THE PARTY AT
www.roalddahl.com

STORIES ARE GOOD FOR YOU.

Roald Dahl said,
*'If you have good thoughts, they will shine
out of your face like sunbeams and you
will always look lovely.'*

We believe in doing good things.
That's why ten per cent of all Roald Dahl income*
goes to our charity partners. We have supported
causes including: specialist children's nurses, grants for
families in need, and educational outreach programmes.
Thank you for helping us to sustain this vital work.

Find out more at roalddahl.com

That's it.
The end of the book.

HERE IS
one LAST **WORD**,
invented by **Roald Dahl**
HIMSELF.
Make sure you KEEP IT SAFE.

SKILLYWIGGLER

Noun: A small creature with big sharp teeth!

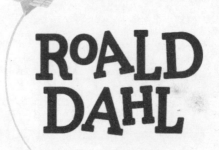